I0654307

Rev. Teeters LeVerge

The AGENT
AND MR. DOBBS

THE SUBGENIUS FOUNDATION
GLEN ROSE 2022

The Agent and Mr. Dobbs by Rev. Teeters LeVerge
Copyright © 2022 Rev. Teeters LeVerge
All rights reserved.

Foreword by Rev. Ivan Stang
Copyright © 2022 Rev. Ivan Stang
All rights reserved.

J. R. "Bob" Dobbs and "SubGenius" are trademarks of
The SubGenius Foundation. All rights reserved.

Cover Design and Interior Design by Rev. Onan Canobite

First Impression: January 2022
The SubGenius Foundation, Glen Rose

LeVerge, Teeters
[English]
Agent and Mr. Dobbs, The
ISBN 978-1-946529-02-2 (limited hardcover)
ISBN 978-1-946529-03-9 (paperback)
1. Wit and Humor
2. Fiction: Visionary and Metaphysical
Rev. Teeters LeVerge (b. 1968); Rev. Ivan Stang (b. 1953)

Defy the sinister star-forces. Evil demons have kept the truth from
humanity for thousands of years. God has been mis-quoted all this
time... His actual words may disturb you.

SubGenius.com

The SubGenius Foundation
P. O. Box 807, Glen Rose, TX 76043 United States

Contents

4

Foreword

Foreword

H. P. Lovecraft by way of Raymond Chandler by way of The Three Stooges.

Don't expect an ending. The story never ends. It's like a hallucinatory dream. The rather demanding proofreading of it alone put me into a profoundly altered state that lasted for days.

Concerning proofreading: you've never seen so many red-pencil marks on a manuscript. The black and white pages now look pink when seen from across a room. Never have I handled a manuscript that was so obviously written in a true frenzy.

Like a David Lynch movie with a dollop of The Trailer Park Boys. Like a Bugs Bunny cartoon guest-directed by David Cronenberg. Like an S. Clay Wilson comic novelized by Franz Kafka.

Rev. Ivan Stang

The Agent
and
Mr. Dobbs

The Agent and Mr. Dobbs

...These papers were found on the body of a transient party clown in the city of Albany, New York in 1989. The papers had been meticulously taped back together after an apparent attempt at shredding them. Some pages are missing. The party clown was determined by the county coroner to have been killed by being force-fed copious amounts of Silly-Putty, some of which still had a cartoon imprint of a pleasant-yet-disturbing face of a smiling man with a pipe clenched between his teeth...

09/05/62

Having picked up the envelope from Agent 614, I proceeded to the rendezvous point at the corners of Maple and White. There as directed I was picked up in a green sedan, model and make indeterminable. I was quickly blindfolded by two men, one of whom was holding a toy cap gun to my side and smiling. It may be important to note that both men had extremely smooth skin on their hands, but also a rank odor about them that belied poor hygiene. There followed a few hours' drive in which I am quite sure we drove in wide circles, for every ten minutes or so we would pop over a bump in the road and the driver would start to giggle and say "Didn't we just pass this a few minutes ago?" and the men in the back with me would start to laugh, mentioning something about the "frop" being really really good that day.

Finally I sensed we were nearing our destination, for the men started to whisper; well, it wasn't quite a whisper, it was more like they were trying to whisper but just couldn't understand the concept of a whisper. I do believe they were speaking in code. They were saying something about "Lets pack another one real quick" and "I dunno, I'm pretty 'fropped' out right now" and "Man, I want some fried prairie squid."

The car stopped and the man to my right yanked off my blind fold. When my eyes finally adjusted to the light I noticed that he was staring at me with bloodshot vacant eyes and a strange smile on his face. We sat like this staring at each other for quite a few tense minutes as his head tilted to the side until he finally "snapped" out of it and got out of the car, ushering me after him. He pointed to a high concrete wall that surrounded a large, well manicured lawn and a very large mansion. He told me to "just knock on the door." I took it to mean knock on the door of the mansion and proceeded up to it. When I turned around, the car I was just in was full of an odd colored smoke, and inane laughter emanated from a slightly open window.

The knocker on the huge oaken front doors was a rather heavy rusty iron piece in the shape of a $. I banged it down thrice and awaited an answer. Soon the door creaked open and in front of me stood the tallest colored man I have ever seen. Even taller than Agent 541. However he had a very high squeaky voice that resembled a certain cartoon mouse. He asked me my business and I replied that I had an urgent appointment with Mr. Dobbs. He seemed fairly out of it too and replied back that the sky was "pretty damn blue today." I had to wait a few minutes until he asked me my business again, but before I could answer he was ushering me into the cavernous building.

Once inside I noticed that it was rather well appointed with both new and antique furnishings, which to my eye seemed to come from all corners of the earth and were set about in no discernible pattern. There were piles of papers and stacks of money everywhere. What caught my eye though was the incredible amount of junk laying about the place. This Mr. Dobbs, it would seem, has a habit of collecting useless objects found by the side of the road.

Finally, after walking through many hallways, I was shown to a door and told to walk in, that I was expected. I did as told. The room I entered was the most sane that I had so far seen — a typical den that any well cultured man may have in his home. Mr. Dobbs was sitting in a large leather armchair with his back to me, a billow of smoke coming up from his front. I slowly walked over to him. He said nothing but with his right hand he motioned me to sit on a metal folding chair adjacent to him. He seemed to be engrossed in a television program, it was *Leave it to Beaver,* a wholesome program.

Suddenly he began to speak: "I do love this show, that Ward Cleaver is one relaxed man. Connie doesn't like me to watch this program, she thinks it's pornographic, but that's why I like it." He fell into a deep silence intently watching a commercial and nodding his head in time with the jingle. When the commercial ended he turned to me and asked "What can I do for you, young agent?"

I noticed then that even though the upper half of his body was clad in a dark suit with white shirt and dark tie, the bottom half of his body was clad only in wing tip shoes. It was very disturbing and put me off for a moment, but I had been warned by my handlers that this Mr. Dobbs had many tricks up his sleeve, and I took this as his way of making a person uncomfortable.

I regained my composure and told him "Mr. Dobbs, the Agency I work for has a request for you," when suddenly Mr. Dobbs got up out of his chair and walked over to a well appointed wet bar and poured a tumbler full of what he claimed was the finest scotch, saying it was from Malaysia or Canada or somewhere. My memory begins to get hazy here. It was not scotch at all; it smelled like grape but tasted for the life of me like gasoline. He bade me to drink. Knowing that he is an important partner I tried to force down a sip.

Then Mr. Dobbs did the strangest thing. He started to do what I believe is called a Hula dance, yet he was humming some tango to himself. Even though I was warned about his eccentric behavior I can not abide a half-naked man dancing in front of, yet I was transfixed by this strange behavior. I know now that I must have been drugged. He danced for a while too close to me for my waning comfort. My heart beat faster and the rank smoke from his pipe seemed to make my head swim and my vision fade. I thought that I was about to faint, when my heart nearly burst as I felt a pair of hands start to message my shoulders. I looked up to see a beautiful blonde with a perfect perm smiling down on me. It took this to be his wife Connie.

She said, "Don't fret... "Bob" likes to dance on Fridays." She continued, "Now now, deary, we mustn't fuck with our company." Mr. Dobbs ignored her and continued his lewd dance. Connie bade me to ask "Bob" what questions I may need to ask him. I started out by getting straight to the point, reminding him of the troubles with Cuba. Mr. Dobbs then did the queerest thing I had seen him do yet. He ran over to a big wooden box on the bar, opened it and pulled out a huge novelty cigar. He then proceeded to insert said huge novelty cigar up his anus. The cigar spontaneously ignited and Mr. Dobbs blew smoke rings out of his ears. Surely this was an illusion or a hallucination from my drugged state. I found myself mesmerized by Mr. Dobbs' antics, Connie's back rub, and the "scotch" that I found myself taking a liking to. Connie's hands reached down to my crotch as I watched Mr. Dobbs preach about economics and Cuba and war, and how it all tied in together, all the while bent over with a huge cigar puffing away in his anus. That is the last I remember of that evening. The ensuing lie detector tests and truth serums have borne that out.

I awoke the next morning, late I believe, with a cool breeze fluttering through pastel pink curtains. I had the worst hangover that I have ever experienced. I can not fully describe the sensation. It was somewhere between getting a root canal and the high of three martinis. I was startled to notice that Connie Dobbs was lying nude next to me. I tried getting up but soon regretted it by the dizziness it caused, and worst of all by what I saw lying next to Connie. All I saw was its shoulders and a cheap bouffant wig on its head. Its skin was gray. I don't mean sickly human gray, I mean gray as gray can be. Its body shape was all out of whack too. Then I had fleeting memories of a wild sexual encounter with Mrs. Dobbs and *something else* I remember having intercourse with orifices that were *not human.* I must have shuddered, for Connie rolled over and picked up a glass of some clear liquid from off the night stand and two tablets. She demanded I take them for they would make me feel better. I inspected the tablets and, though they resembled your basic aspirin, they had embossed on them the word "Pils." Afraid of being drugged again I tried to hide them in my cheek, but when I drank that liquid, they just slid down my throat. Within minutes reality started to fade and some sort of orgy began. The last thing I remember was Mr. Dobbs dressed as a clown, with no pants on of course, attempting to take my virginity. I still have nightmares about this, but as they say, "My Country Right or Wrong."

Weeks passed of which I have little memory. I know this only because of the date on which I was retrieved by The Agency. The Dobbses and their minions kept me pretty well "Fropped Up" as they called it.

The next event that I have any clear memory of was of taking a ridiculously long elevator ride deep into the earth at the BobCo Mining and Soylent Green Consortium in Wyoming. We must have been on that elevator for three hours. One of Dobbs' minions had taken my watch during the "orgy" and refused to give it back, saying that "Bob" doesn't pay enough and he had to get some "stuff" for a weekend party he and the Kennedys were having with one Doctor Oswald.

When we finally alighted from the elevator, to my surprise we were not in some mine shaft as I expected, but in a huge vaulted warehouse full of novelty goods that were being stacked and sorted by strange short "men" shrouded in sack rags. "Bob" claimed that they were ex-Nazis scientists working on some "super-dooper-extra secret" project for the government. I could clearly see that they were not men at all but slaves of some unknown species. By this time I had found it to my better judgment not to doubt Mr. Dobbs, at least out loud.

We took a golf cart type of vehicle down a long winding corridor. Mr. Dobbs not once paid any attention to where he was driving. He decided to, at that time, ramble on and on about some mysterious substance he called "Slack," all the while puffing insanely on his pipe, the bowl of which soon glowed a bright red. During this journey we ran over three of "Bob's" slave-men and nearly hit countless others. Mr. Dobbs was oblivious to each "accident." I put that in quotes, for each one of the slaves, I happened to notice, had been pointing a weapon of some sort at Mr. Dobbs right before he mindlessly ran over them. This mysterious Mr. Dobbs may have some sort of "second sight" or is just incredibly lucky. As you will see, I believe it has more to do with luck and some sort of strange "time control" powers than anything else.

Mr. Dobbs' underground office was a horror. I barely can describe it. It was a total mess and stank of the tobacco that he constantly smoked. In fact, I never saw Mr. Dobbs without that infernal pipe clenched between his teeth. It was only after a few minutes of adjusting to the stench and mess of the office that I truly saw what the room held, and it horrified me. The place had severed human heads strewn haphazardly all over. Now, I have seen some terrible sights in my life, and I suspect that if I remain on the Dobbs case I will see worse, but what made me gasp was that the heads were not of random humans but of public figures that we would all recognize. I saw the heads of

This section was carefully cut out of the original report.

and one was actually singing! It begged me in a tenor to "please kill me." Surprisingly, considering the state I was in, I did not faint. Instead, with all the smoke from "Bob's" special tobacco mix, I started to laugh. This got "Bob" all worked up, he started to jump around inanely and laugh with me. He then proceeded to use one of the heads (not the singing head) in a most foul manner.

"Bob" bade me to sit down on a chair that was stacked high with papers. I looked at the stack and back at "Bob," wondering what he expected me to do. By this time I had begun to get in the "spirit" of the situation, and laughingly knocked the stack of papers on the floor. Mr. Dobbs did not seem to mind, in fact he stared down at the mess I made, expressed thanks, and picked up a sheet of paper, saying that he'd been "looking for this contract" for quite some time. The glyphs on the sheet were of no known human alphabet that I have ever encountered. For some reason this worried me and reminded me of the slaves I saw working for "Bob," and that dreadful night with Mrs. Dobbs and that strange gray creature. I did not have much time to consider the implications, for Mr. Dobbs wadded up the paper, tossed it in a corner and told me to follow him. This time we did not take the vehicle but instead walked down dark and dank corridors with a gradual down slope. Being without a timepiece, I can not estimate how long we walked, but it seemed like hours. Here I must admit that my perceptions of time had been warped by constant exposure to "Bob's" tobacco.

II

MR. Dobbs finally guided me to our final destination. What I saw in that final "Circle of Hell" I cannot, I WILL not reveal. Through all the pressure that the Agency could bear against me, a loyal, true blue Agent and American, I found it in OUR best interests to keep some things secret even from the Boss, "the man in the dress." I do this for the good of our nation and out of fear. For what Mr. Dobbs revealed to me was so horrific, so humorous, so bizarre, so unChristian, so baffling and DANGEROUS that I hyperventilated through the inane laughter that was my only defense lest I totally lose my mind. The last thing I remembered of that day was Mr. Dobbs dancing around my prostrate body (he was prancing really) and mimicking my insane laughter with his own even crazier chortles. He spoke no words, he just laughed, but his laughter seemed to speak volumes to my inner mind. I laughed, I wept, I urinated in my undergarments (Mr. Dobbs somehow had relieved me of my slacks, when I do not recall).

I awoke, I am not sure when, on a garbage strewn beach in some tropical or sub-tropical location. I recall the sound of ocean waves breaking on the shore and that of a mambo band. I almost choked when I was offered a Daiquiri by the Dictator F_____ C_____ who was sitting next to me on the beach towel. I drank the beverage only out of a severe thirst. It was tasty, however; you can't beat good C_____ rum. Sitting on the other side of me was Doctor Oswald, who was removing the cash from my wallet, mumbling about "that damn "Bob" never pays me on time." I was so overwhelmed that I did nothing to counter his actions.

F_____ C_____ kept serving me Daiquiris, so in a very short time I found myself intoxicated again. Though my actions may seem un-American, bear in mind that I considered myself still "undercover." I eventually extricated myself by saying I needed to urinate in the ocean.

While doing my business I was startled by Mr. Dobbs shooting up out of the water in front of me like a deranged dolphin, his pipe miraculously still smoking! He mentioned that the water was quite a bit warmer here and if I would not mind if he lingered to warm himself up a bit. I of course never told him of the source of the warmth.

I was startled again by what I initially thought were Mrs. Dobbs' (Connie's) hands rubbing the strain out of my back. "Bob" sat in the water in front of me, smiling, while I felt all the tension being messaged from my shoulders. It was incredibly relaxing until a slim gray hand popped another DobbsCo "Pil" in my mouth and smoothed it down my throat. It was not Mrs. Dobbs, it was that damnable gray creature from that horrible first night at the Dobbs residence.

"Bob" found my confusion and fear amusing. He laughed and jumped up and down in the water, screaming, ""Bob" wants one too! "Bob" wants one too!" Mr. Dobbs received a large handful of "Pils." Strangely they seemed to sober him up, unlike in my case, where the hallucinations began in earnest again — for I could have sworn I saw Mr. Dobbs soon after absentmindedly battling a giant shark while lecturing both F_____ C_____ and Doctor Oswald on the convoluted concept he called "Slack."

The next event I clearly remember was having martinis on a jet with the Mr. and Mrs. Dobbs, *THE* President *and* his wife, and that abominable gray creature. Mr. Dobbs was bemoaning the reliability of Doctor Oswald while the President was assuring him that though he had a tendency to whine about being left out, all in all he was reliable. Mrs. Dobbs, the President's wife and the Gray were divining the future from the entrails of a squid, and all three seemed deeply concerned.

Feeling bold and being sick of the constant drugging that was taking place, I stood up and demanded to know what "really" was going on. Initially I was ignored, until I tried to grab the pipe out of Mr. Dobbs' mouth. It would not budge; it was like it was part of his bone structure, but it did grab his attention. He looked at me straight in the eye, his constant grin seemed to get bigger, and his face dissolved into a mass of tiny luminescent dots. It was then that I knew he had The Power.

I backed away in fear and awe until the President beckoned me over, stuttering in his annoying New England accent, "It's all right, son... "Bob" got things under control." I thought to myself that this buffoon, this magician, this slacker, has things under control?

But it appears that he did/does. I was then quickly "sold" like in an auction, by our President to Mr. Dobbs for a stack of Styrofoam cups, a game of tic-tac-toe, which Mr. Dobbs declared he had to win, and a carefully chosen doughnut from a squished box that lay at the President's feet.

I felt exhausted. I felt that I somehow had let down my country, even though I was in essence commanded by our President to obey Mr. Dobbs. It pained me to think that I was sold to this Man-God-Beast for some junk. Then I remembered my oath. Then I remembered all the junk lying around Mr. Dobbs' mansion. The severed heads. I was just a part of a bigger plan. I knew then it was my duty to "play the game through." Still, my insides burned with shame. For the rest of the flight I sat brooding. Nothing could bring me out of my funk, not Mr. Dobbs' childish and obvious magic coin tricks (I knew very well he had it in his hand when he'd pulled the quarter from behind my ear). Neither could the President's poor impersonations of cartoon characters pull me from my funk. It was only the "Pils" that got me in the swing of things, and that was a shame to me in and of itself.

The Dobbses, the Gray and I were dropped off in Miami Beach where the Dobbs' had a residence, while the President mentioned that he had to go to some "secret" base in New Mexico until "things cooled down a bit."

The Dobbs' Florida residence was not at all like their mansion. It was small and neat. I was ushered into the bathroom and told to take a shower for, according to "Bob," I smelled "like the Elder Ones on a fucking binge." The shower immediately sobered me up and I found that I was famished. Dinner, however, was a disappointment. It was cold rice with a bit of rat meat. "Bob" said he learned this hangover remedy from one "Uncle Ho" and that I'd "better get used to it." It was disgusting, I feigned eating, hiding the half-chewed scraps in my napkin. "Bob" did not eat but puffed away on his pipe. Connie, however, ate with gusto. After "dinner" I insisted that we go to a Tiki Lounge that I knew of nearby for ham and pineapple. I told them that it was on me (though I had no cash after Doctor Oswald's thievery). This excited "Bob" to such a degree that he jumped up on the table and started to do his "Friday Night Dance" again. It took Connie some time to quiet him down.

20

III

"BOB" decided that we would walk while Connie would take their pedicab. I had never seen a pedicab service here in our Great Nation. Although I was beginning to feel immune to the insanity that permeated my experiences around the Dobbses, I actually vomited a little in my mouth when I saw the creature that was pulling the pedicab. It was A_____ H_____! His mustache was shaved but it was *him*! I could see the stitch mark scars around the top of his head where his brain had been *reinserted*! I was always led to believe that the Soviets burned his body, but sold his brain to us in exchange for The Secret that "those folks we found in R_____ N.M." sold to us in exchange for the bodies of their comrades. What a revelation! As is known, I lost my big brother to the Germans in The Big One, so every cell in my body wanted to strangle that terrible thing standing by the curb — but seeing him dressed in a tutu with rabbit ears on his head, I was moved to pity. It was quite obvious that he was near brain-dead at this point. He could also, I might add, haul that pedicab pretty damn fast in those six-inch stiletto heels.

Further down the sidewalk on that moonlit, humid night, I had to finally admit to "Bob" that Doctor Oswald had stolen all my money. "Bob" snickered and nodded knowingly, saying, "Hehehe, he is a little worm, but I have plans for him." I was pondering this potentially dangerous comment when "Bob" suddenly stopped and bent down to tie his shoe. I continued walking ahead when a brick from nowhere hit me squarely in the head. Thank God for the steel plate I had placed there after The "Accident," for if "Bob" had not stopped to tie his shoe, I am sure he might have been brained — though now I wonder if he could ever be hurt; he has the most persistent luck of any man I have ever known. When "Bob" had finished tying his shoe (ignoring my yelps of pain and the blood violently flowing down my face) he stood back up holding someone's lost wallet. Miraculously, he said that he knew its owner, one Dr. Tim Leary. It would seem that they were old friends. "Bob" mumbled to himself that the S.O.B. owed him as he proceeded to take from the wallet all the cash, a "Sandal Warehouse" charge card, and a folded slightly blue tinted piece of paper that was perforated into many small squares. This object "Bob" seemed most excited about, for he shoved it into his mouth and mumbled something like "Let them try to read *my* mind again." He then started to chuckle. He chuckled until we walked into the Tiki Lounge. At least we now had over $100.00 in cash.

Connie was already seated at a table with two "cabana boys" dancing for her. "Bob" took me by the arm and led me up to the bar, where he filled one hand with colorful Monopoly money and the other with a wad of a strange-smelling sticky "tobacco" and a chewed up old pipe. He told me to "frop up a bit 'n get somethin' to drink." He glared over at Connie, hitched up his pants and mumbled that he "had to take care of things" and "those damn cabana boys stole my dance moves."

I found myself engrossed in this strange "tobacco." It was not what the youth of today call "maryjane;" it had a foul odor and taste, but for some reason I found that it not only soothed my spirit but the pipe seemed to be stuck in my mouth. I was not clenching my teeth down on the stem, yet I could not extract it! It was as if it had glued itself to my mouth. That made eating dinner rather difficult. I was becoming oblivious under the influence of this "weed" when I heard the sounds of breaking glass. I knew it must be "Bob." Sure enough, he had pushed all the plates and glasses off the table and was dancing with the cabana boys on the table top. Connie looked away in apparent disgust as she filed her nails with what looked like the severed hand of a gorilla or some other sort of Great Ape.

"Bob" then threw a salt shaker which hit me directly in the forehead, causing it to bleed. I must add that no one had mentioned that my face was already covered in fresh blood, or that I was not wearing trousers; "Bob" had not given them back to me yet. He yelled to me, "Get those damn Mai Tais... I have a powerful thirst!" I proffered the Monopoly money to the bartender in my "fropped up" state; he looked at "Bob" and back to me, shook his head and produced a pitcher of the drink. There was fear in his eyes. Is this "Bob" a member of "the criminal group that does not exist?"

It may have been some strange influence of the "frop," but the twenty feet and the few seconds that it took to get to our table

seemed more like a mile and an hour. I wonder now if there was
not some sort of space/time distortion brought on by the "frop,"
for when I arrived at the table, it was neatly set with plates of
appetizers which very much looked and tasted like flambéed monkey
brains. "Bob's" were raw. Already seated was a youngish looking
man who was introduced as "Timmy-Boy." "Bob" said that he had
"big jumbo big giant colossal plans" for him. This was apparently
the same Dr. Tim Leary whose wallet "Bob" had just found on the
street! I began to wonder if I were being set up, but reviewing the
strange luck that "Bob" seemed to have, I had to admit to myself
that maybe this guy was more than extraordinary. He already had
shown that he had at least as much power as the President.

"Bob" did give Dr. Leary his back his wallet, but claimed that
some "young punks" jumped us. He pointed convincingly to my
bloody head and shirt, stating that my bleeding head was "good."
I still don't understand what he meant by that. Dr. Leary tore
through his wallet in an angry manner. He grabbed "Bob" by the
wrist, stating, not asking, "You took the blotter?" "Bob" just stuck
out his tongue with the messy, faded and chewed wad of paper
sitting upon it. His tongue was extraordinary long and lizard-like.
He snapped it back in with a grin. Dr. Leary drew his hands back
to himself and pouted.

Dinner went surprisingly well. The conversation was adept and
civilized, though the Dobbses seemed to have a language of their
own which Dr. Leary and I could somehow follow. The only two
disconcerting issues I remembered was that every time I tried to
pour a drink for myself, "Bob" would knock it out of my hands,
stating, "Frop before booze, you can't lose; booze after frop, you'll
wish you were fucking dead." The other issue I had was that what
I thought was Connie's smooth hand rubbing my knee (she is a
knock-out!) was, however, of course, not hers — and no, it was not
the "gray's" either. It was that damn A_____ H_____ under the
table begging for scraps. I kicked the thing away, but out of mercy
did give it the cold monkey brains that I could not finish. This
"frop" has the odd ability to make one hungry, but to, at the same
time, make the act of eating very very strange and uncomfortable.
I could chew the food but was unable to swallow it. "Bob" on the
other hand did eat heartily: half a pig, all the raw monkey brains, a

light bulb (I do not know where he got it), the tropical flowers set in the table, and what I fear to think was a human heart... raw.

A_____ H_____ had to pull us all back to the Dobbs' bungalow in the pedicab. I did not pity him at that point. During the whole trip back "Bob" kept looking up at the night skies, pointing out constellations that were not there, muttering "Gort Klaatu Veranda Nixon." Whatever was in the monkey brains he ate certainly seemed to have relaxed him, for when we got back to the house and discovered that the "gray" had messed it up while we were out to dinner, "Bob" seemed peeved yet accepted the situation with grace. He put some very strange music on the hi-fi, lounged back into an easy chair and lectured me. I quote as best I can remember:

"Young man, Thous hast muchly to un-learn. I sayest thus out of *pure* spite. Thou hast dis-understood everything I havest revealedest to thouest, which in mine eyes is un-re-un-nerving... and thou dost FUCK me over?"

I replied, "Mr. Dobbs, I was sent on a mission that you requested. I have only held back one truth, which is that you are a wanted man... wanted by our Great Nation to smite our enemies. I was told that you have the powers to do that. Then why don't you?"

"Bob" wriggled around in his chair, I feared another dance session coming on, but he seemed un-"Bob"-fully nervous. "Look, you little monkey boy, I just ate the brains of your great-great-great uncle with a bit of lime juice. Do you want to De-Re-Un-Evolve back to our natural state, or *evolve into a pile of ashes*?"

I sat staring at his classical face, pondering what he had told (not asked) me. His face and body began to shimmer, flickering like a film projector gone haywire. "Bob" scrunched his face up and let out a fart that literally shook the house. This emission propelled him up in the air to the point of hitting his head on the ceiling, then he slowly descended back to the exact spot at which he had previously been sitting. A change had come over him: his eyes had glassed over, and he looked confused, as might an elderly man with dementia. "So," he said out of the blue, "Lets get some hookers! I know of a great place next to Cape Canaveral."

IV

"BOB" drove, if one could even call it driving, for he never once had his hands on the wheel; he appeared to steer with his knees, but mostly with another part of his anatomy that seemed to have a literal mind of its own (at least according to Connie). "Bob" never looked out the windshield. The whole time he was behind the wheel he had his head sticking out the driver's side window, nostrils flared to an incredible degree and his tongue hanging out like a dog's. I myself had my foot pushed hard on the floor against a nonexistent foot brake and my hands clenched on the door handle. "Bob" was constantly looking around and up into the night skies. He said he was "looking for *Them* and *psniffing* [he pronounced it 'Pah-Sniffin'] around for the Skunk Ape" — a version, he told me, of the Himalayan Yeti. He said there were many of them around this part of Florida, that they were friendly, but had glands that contained a powerful aphrodisiac — "... so either way, if you run into one, you get lucky."

It was not long until he slammed on the brakes and we skidded off into a ditch. "Bob" bounded out of the car and started to run into a swampy area to the west. I followed out of stupidity, for the bramble and the vines growing in the swamp cut my legs up badly. (I still had no trousers.) I should mention that "Bob" did not actually run, he leapt and bounded more like a gazelle, quite gracefully. When I finally caught up with him he was rolling around in a large patch of trampled-down cane that certainly looked like the bedding of a Great-Ape-like creature. The smell was sickening, but did have a strange allure to it. "Bob" was in ecstasy as he rolled around in the stinking muck. "Must be in heat!" he exclaimed as he got up; oddly his clothing had not one speck of dirt or mud on it! When I mentioned that, he just giggled, and for the first time acknowledged that I was wearing no trousers, saying, "We'll have to remedy that."

Once we were back in the car, "Bob" let out a sigh that sounded almost sad. "Skunk Ape is one hot-to-trot Yeti." He whispered something in a strange language to himself as he played "pocket pool" in his pants. "Well, now, son... off to get you some trousers."

We had not driven far, maybe a mile, to the edge of a small rundown town, full of "white trash" as they say in the South. "Bob's" nostrils started to flare again as he "psniffed" about in the air and chuckled to himself. We pulled off onto the side of the road next to a ramshackle house that was more down than up. The incongruity was not lost on me, at least: "Bob" dressed to a T with his battleship-sized Cadillac, compared to this hovel before which we were parked. However, "Bob" showed no sign of noticing; he simply knocked on the door. Soon a much degraded man of indeterminate age answered. "Bob," without introductions, offered to sell this man a haircut in exchange for the incredibly filthy overalls he was wearing. The degenerate hillbilly agreed to the deal without haggling. In fact I would say that he seemed ecstatic. He practically swooned.

The haircut "Bob" gave him was perfect. He even styled it exactly like his own, using hair gel from a tube he had in his jacket pocket. He emphatically told the man, "*Now* things are going to change for the better." Admittedly, I did see "Bob" absentmindedly place one hand on a rickety wooden shelf and grab what looked like a government check, while with the other he regally proffered the man a five-cent plastic comb, grinning as if he just done him a favor. I don't think Mr. Dobbs is a thief per se, nor a kleptomaniac; he may simply not have control over himself and his desires in the same way that we normal people do. For myself, I am glad that I did not have a mirror to see myself so shamefully dressed: my standard jacket, tie, white shirt, wing tip shoes — and the filthiest, smelliest pair of overalls that could be imagined. "Bob" took an uncomfortably close "pwhiff" of me and nodded his approval. "Hmmmm, *now you smell useful...*"

Again, I must emphasize that this Man is by nature uncanny and Powerful! He is a force to be either feared or harnessed, if that is even possible, and I doubt that it is. I have a gut feeling that *we* may find it advantageous to adapt ourselves to *him*.

With "Bob" driving well over eighty miles per hour, we made it to the Cape Canaveral area quickly. By this time I had given up on worrying and had decided to follow whatever path Mr. Dobbs might drag me down, for it occurred to me that so far, despite all the experiences I had been through, I had suffered little permanent physical damage. Mental damage, on the other hand, was possibly extreme... maybe. I say "maybe" for I think I was beginning to understand this incredible man and his "wisdom"... if one can ever say that Mr. Dobbs can be understood, at least with our stunted minds.

Instead of the expected whorehouse, we drove to a large modern factory in sight of Cape Canaveral. "Bob" said that it was one of his "dis-embodiment" stations and that he "had to go number 3." I assumed that he meant that he needed to defecate, but was drunk and misspoke.

The factory, "Bob" told me, made a substance call "Dumb-Ass-Putty." The substance they produced worked in the same way as the child's plaything "Silly Putty" — but was an utter failure, "Bob" told me, because of the extreme toxicity of the materials used (and I also assume because of its name). Mr. Dobbs did not lament the ongoing failure; he shrugged it off, saying something about "a few less pinks," "possible good mutations" and "a huge tax write off." This Man is sinister, but this Man may be our only hope. I shall explain why later in the report.

For a toy factory it had better security than I had seen even at our Base X. Not only were there twenty-foot concrete walls topped with embedded glass and razor wire, there were guard posts every five feet so that the guards could pass notes and "pipes" back and forth. Even "Bob" was I.D.ed at the entrance, which was more akin to the heavy gates that lead into a castle than anything. He even had a moat around it with what looked like alligators. (They, I eventually leaned, turned out to be alligator *people*, the cast-offs from one of BobCo's genetic enhancement laboratories!)

This factory was like none I had ever seen. Sure, there were huge machines pushing out some putty-like substance into large vats that oddly had stenciled on them "Tuna Surprise" — and come to think of it, the "food" canning part of the factory had machines with the same title stenciled on them as well. However I was shocked when "Bob" led me into a room the size of an aircraft carrier, filled with the most advanced computers I had ever seen. There were hundreds if not thousands of Nancy Reagan (*nee* Davis) look-alikes pushing punch cards into the slots!

"Bob" and I walked through the cavernous affair, me with my mouth agape and "Bob" with his typical grin — that is, until he slapped one of the women on the behind. His hand bounced back, wrapped around his mid-section as if it were made of *rubber* and smacked him on the back of the head. He glared at the woman and coughed as a key then shot out of his mouth! He rubbed the back of his head as he picked it up, telling me, "807 is a feisty one" and "Hmmmm, I thought I'd lost this key." It was same key he'd used to unlock his office door! Here, the office, in contrast to the other one I saw before, was well appointed and typical for a powerful executive.

"Bob" sat himself down behind a large desk and gathered up huge, neatly piled stacks of papers. He then very deliberately laid them on the floor in two piles. One pile he dove into and rolled around in vigorously. When he got up he smoothed his suit, breathing heavily. He told me that those particular contracts *would* be signed. *"They"* could no longer refuse them. Then he got an all fours and snuffled around the other pile like a hound dog. Using his tongue he pulled out a few sheets, undid the zipper on his pants, lifted a leg and urinated on them. These were the ones, he told me, that *he* had just signed. Sure enough, as if an invisible ink were being revealed, "J. R. "Bob" Dobbs, esq." slowly appeared on the papers, albeit in thick child-like handwriting. "Bob," exhausted, then lay down to take a nap, but only after making sure that he had securely locked me into the room. I could not be sure at first if he were exactly asleep, for he lay down with his arms to his side, stiff as a board, like a corpse. I was sure he was trying to fool me somehow. It wasn't until he started "passing gas" like a snorer would snore that I took the opportunity to search the room. The papers (I dared not touch the befouled ones) were standard contracts though some seemed to speak of deals for human flesh, human souls, and unimaginably vast amounts of money. His desk, however was filled with cotter pins, broken pens and jars of urine. I am sure it was urine, for each one was labeled "PeE (a date) J.R." and a little note: "Good Vintage, a little salty though," "removes assouls," "Bad Day," and so on. One drawer was entirely filled with money clips. The one below it was filled with *severed and dried human hands*! I reeled in fear for at that exact moment, "Bob" mumbled loudly in his sleep *"You are next, boy!"*

Forgetting that I had long lost the trousers of my own, I reached into the pockets of the filthy overalls and pulled out, not any kind of practical weapon as I had hoped for, but instead a diamond-encrusted money clip that contained hundreds of dollars. I backed up against the wall as "Bob" rose and came toward me with glowing red eyes that seemed filled not with greed, but with an animal-like lust, his ever-present grin wider, bigger, and scarier than ever. He pinned me there; his breath smelled like a mix between fresh paint and garlic. His breathing was heavy, frightening. He took one hand down and slipped the money clip from my limp fingers saying, "This is mine. I gave the haircut." This was the first time that I was truly afraid of what Mr. Dobbs might do to me. Even though he grinned, his lifeless eyes (or maybe eyes *too* full of life) spoke of some abyss, of *some thing* that I could never understand. He then brought his pipe filled lips next to my ear. The sizzling of the "tobacco" in it sounded like bacon, but smelled like some used diaper that had been forgotten in a defunct rubber factory. The vomit rose in my throat. He whispered to me to look in the "Forbidden Drawer." Having no idea what drawer that would be, I pulled a random drawer out of a file cabinet adjacent to myself. My hand rummaged around in it while my eyes remained fixed on his. I extracted a stack of papers and pulled them close to me. Every sheet had a few typewritten lines on them. I tried to focus on them. To my relief, they were all bad (very bad) one-liner jokes of the kind that you hear at cheap burlesque houses. "Bob" glared at me, his grin becoming sinister (or should I say *more* sinister?)... yet I must admit his gaze was hypnotizing. This was the first time I dared look so deeply into his eyes. Relief came only when he loosened his grip on me, chuckled, and said, if I remember correctly, "Seen mah secret stash, head didn't explode... passed the test." I relaxed a little and leaned against the wall, sweating profusely. "Bob" rhythmically nodded his head as if to some tune that he could only hear. "Now Ye shallest gazest uponest the timelessest ofest the mostest grusomestest of horrorseseses." Again he tried (and failed) to sound "Biblical," yet now I wondered, that if, perhaps, the ancients in the Good Book had not spoken with an affected drawl. This "Bob" was obviously not of our realm as we know it; or, he may just be semi-retarded and very very lucky.

He ushered me into a room filled with junk that he called "Bull-dada." I assumed, what with all the Bobco "pils" that he had been popping, he meant DaDa "art." Seriously, it was junk. Old balls of carefully wound used and dirty string, newspaper and magazine clippings of male models (oddly they all looked like "Bob"), poorly painted monster movie plastic models, and greenish stone figurines of strange looking sea creatures. Mr. Dobbs put his hand on my shoulder and gestured widely with his other hand as if I should appreciate some great treasure of art. I still don't understand his pride with that room of junk, nor what I should "greatly fearest" about it all. It is still a mystery to me.

It was apparently time to go, for "Bob," after wiping a tear from his eye, said "I must attend to 'bidness'" as he guided me down a long fluorescent-lit hallway. It was then that I noted, in my sobriety, that he seemed to be floating a fraction of an inch *off the ground* That would explain the lack of dirt that ever sullied his person. But it may also explain his luck. I suspect he is too stupid to recognize his own mortality (let alone the fact that he is walking and that gravity matters), so that just like the leader of that Russian pre-Soviet "spiritual" movement Bulatovism, "Bob" just breezes through the act of living, never worrying or contemplating his next (or any) movement. He may be too mentally "special" to understand even in the most basic way that *rules apply.*

We came to a door with the words "Janitor Place" crudely painted on it. I sighed, thinking it was just another of "Bob's" ruses to get me alone... again. However when he opened the door I was nearly blinded by bright lights. It was no janitor closet. It opened to a huge research center that would put our efforts to great shame. There were hundreds of men, women and *things* in white lab coats, all scratching away at chalk boards, squinting over slide rules, arguing, generally looking like brilliant scientists. I have little understanding of Zero Gravity Physics, but from what I saw of our quick walk-through, these people and things were onto something *big.* "Bob" seemed quite unimpressed; in fact he pushed me along saying, "I really, *really* need to go number three."

We arrived at a sealed doorway. "Bob" pushed aside a few feeble "grays" as he inserted his head inside a vertical toilet-looking device. He groaned with pleasure as he turned the pages of a cheap monster movie magazine with his toes. I repeat, I do not know what he did with his head in that device, but I do know that he said, "Takin' a number 3 is better than psex." Mr. Dobbs seemed much relieved after taking this "number 3." He had more of his trademarked relaxed self about him. He even gave me back the money clip (sans the diamonds and cash) and patted me on the shoulder like a benevolent father. The clip did contain a piece of paper that in his childish scrawl said "IOU stuff."

This incredible factory seemed to have no end. We wandered for miles, it would seem, with "Bob" either admiring his image that shone from his highly polished shoes, or flipping a quarter that always landed on its edge — about which he seemed a little ticked off. "Bob" nonchalantly opened a regular looking steel door that led into a huge playground-like room filled with primates!

These were no ordinary primates. They all wore lab coats, business suits, party dresses; some even dressed like Harlem Hep Cat pimps! All these primates were most definitely busy at work of all sorts. Equations were being written on blackboards, martinis were being deftly made by the females of the group, the business ones were hunched, brows knotted with stress, over little desks, scribbling away with fountain pens. However, every once in awhile they would all drop their stumpy trousers, defecate, and throw the feces at one another, shrieking high pitched screams. "Bob" said that he liked to come here to relax, especially after doing a number three. "They know *exactly* what they do!" "Bob" made a gesture — all too real, with sound effects — of defecating and throwing feces. "I likes it!" he declared. His grin got wider as he too jumped up and down like the primates, mimicking their movements and voices. He bounded around the large room amongst them, in essence becoming one of them. And, yes, he did defecate and throw his feces around. And yet... it made sense!

V

A FTER all the "monkey bidness," as "Bob" called it, he was in a much better mood. I suppose all that man needs is to take a number 3 and fling a bit of feces around to "even his keel." His grin was radiant as we walked out to into the hot humid night. We tarried around his car for a few minutes. These were the most relaxed moments that I'd had with Mr. Dobbs up to this point. I offhandedly asked him for a cigarette, and though I had never seen him smoke anything but his infernal pipe, he pulled a pack of my favorite brand of smokes (Ol' Tar Lung) from his jacket pocket. It was a needed smoke, one that I had not enjoyed since I was rotated back from Korea in '52. "Bob" smiled at my obvious joy, telling me, "Those coffin nails sure make a tasty cancer in you Pinks... spread it on my fresh sliced human-pain-toast every mornin'." "Bob" then hopped like a drunken rabbit into the driver's side of the vehicle and shouted to me. "Now, we gonna have some *real* good fun, boy. Get in... *now*." He then let out the most outrageously poor simulation of a "rebel yell" that I have ever heard. It sounded more like the mating call of those Great Apes that reside in deepest darkest Congo. It reverberated through the thick night air. I think I may have heard a call in response... but it could have been just a drunken red-neck.

We sped off down a semi-hidden dirt road that ran behind his toy-and-tuna-factory/genetic/aerospace research center. The vines and leaves hung low as we whipped down this lane, so low and sharp that my face quickly became a mass of scratches. "Bob" would occasionally look over at me and leer, telling me in an oily voice. "You're looking sweeter by the minute." My heart was in my throat, not only because of the insane driving, but also because I feared that "Bob" might have other, more perverted plans for me. This seemed too painfully real of a possibility to me, for "Bob" started to sniff the air lustfully and play "pocket pool" again... vigorously.

After a few tense moments for me — Mr. Dobbs was cool as a "perverted cucumber" the whole time — we finally slid to a halt in front of what I can only describe as the most stinking, rundown, decrepit roadhouse ever to sit in the middle of nowhere. It was truly a ramshackle affair. Half of the neon signs had only a letter or two lit up, there was a huge pile of smelly trash out front (I discerned *humanoid* skulls in the pile),and the peeling paint said it all. The structure's sign dangled off to one side, reading, "Ye Olde Exist Bar & Grille."

If the outside was a shambles, then the inside was worse. It smelled like a cheap brewery that had been forgotten in an open sewer since the reign of Ashurnasirpol II. I wondered why the hell "Bob," a man of such wealth that he could easily afford to frequent any of the finest clubs in Florida, would take me here. It then occurred to me that this might just be *the* whorehouse. When we walked into the joint, the whole place erupted with drunken shouts of "Bob!" — and, for some reason, "JAR!" I stood amazed, for the clientele was astounding by anybody's standard. I saw John Birch *passionately* kissing Mao Tze Tung in one corner; I saw our V_____ P_____ rubbing the crotch of the preserved corpse of Stalin while drunkenly shouting about "Goddamn pinko faggots!" I witnessed Emma Goldman's disembodied head *screaming The International*, I saw M_____ M_____ stabbing (as I was later to learn) our *actual* (non-cloned!) President in the right eye with a fork while Frank Sinatra groveled at her feet. There were also

Rest of the page blanked out.

and the young folk singer Bob Dylan! Richard Attenborough was filming it all.

The worst part, however, were the "whores" in the joint: Grays, Greens, Mauves, Reptilians, Anti-Reptilians, *"Them"* and others that I did not recognize. All were gaudily dressed as housewives, construction workers, maids, business men, house painters, B-Girls, dead astronauts... the list goes on... and all wore horribly cheap bouffant wigs. "Bob" handed me a jar of yellowish fluid and a handful of "Pils," telling me that he would soon be back. He took a dozen of the "whores" upstairs with him, winking sickeningly at me. I swallowed the "Pils" dry.

When "Bob" eventually made it back down to the bar where I had seated myself, sipping a cheap beer, his face was all aglow; literally, it shone green then red. One of those gray creatures was behind the bar pouring a jelly jar full of "vodka" for Premier Khrushchev! "Bob" sat down between us. He still had a satisfied grin on his face that smacked of unknowable pleasures. "Bob" suggested that we have a drinking contest. The "Pils" were really kicking in at this point, so I found it hard to believe my eyes, but it was even harder to *deny* what I was actually seeing.

"This is... our... place... the... real... place where... things get done..." he whispered to me. Then, speaking directly to the Premier of the Soviet Union, he said, "So, Nickie! Think you can drink me under the table tonight, eh?" Khrushchev looked "Bob" straight in the eye, something I had seen very few attempt. "Yesh Meester Doobs, I drink until you, how you say, blow O-ring." The gray then passed "Bob," Khrushchev and I each a full jelly jar of "vodka." Both Khrushchev and "Bob" downed theirs. Halfway through mine I had to run outside to vomit. I swear it was paint thinner; the label on the bottle had "Paint Thinner" crossed out and "Vodka" written underneath. My original guess of it being moonshine was awfully wrong.

When I stumbled back in bleary eyed, I bumped into none other than Richard M. Nixon. Even if my eyes were blurred, I could not mistake his voice. He cursed me as he chased a small dog around. I made my weaving way back up to the bar, where "Bob" and "Nickie" were now glaring and laughing manically at each other while pounding their shoes on the bar top. It would seem that "Bob" had won the Paint Thinner drinking contest, for as I sat down on my stool, Khrushchev's eyes rolled to the back of his head and he fell off his bar stool onto the sodden floor and into oblivion. I was horrified, and asked "Bob" if he were all right, for this could potentially be a World Destructive Event. Mr. Dobbs told me, "He's fine, the little tyke. He'll be ready for another one in the morning... but first, young Agent, let us have a snack."

I feared that suggestion of food, for my stomach was still in knots from being sick, but "Bob" nonetheless led me to a long table that was covered with all manner of edibles — if you dare call them that. There was a bucket of small red colored balls of a gelatinous material that "Bob" told me was "prairie squid caviar." It smelled like rotten fish bait. I had to run back outside to be sick again. "Bob" seemed to relish them, for he ate the whole large bucketful with his grimy hands. He let out a belch and for some reason rubbed his back side. I vomited harder at *that* stench.

When I made it back inside, worse for the wear, "Bob" told me that we wanted to try his luck (!) at one of the many card tables. The rest of the evening was a horrible blur, for not only did he force-feed me "Pils" but he kept buying round after round of the local (actual) moonshine (thank God). Mr. Dobbs could hold his "likker" well, though he did seem to flicker *bodily* on and off like a broken television, especially when he did poorly at the games of chance. At one point we — "Bob," Mao, Churchill, a Beatnik type, Ed Sullivan, a strangle alien looking creature with the face of a cuttlefish and I — were playing some sort of complicated card game wherein the cards themselves represented different currencies, *worlds*, and... immortal souls....

"Bob" lost the last big hand of the night. In a rare fit of anger he snatched the cards from the "alien" and threw them onto the floor, cursing, "Well, I do believe that I've been cheated!" He then grabbed from the table (wrong side up it seemed to me) an IOU written on a bar napkin and squinted his drunken eyes at it, saying, "I guess I'll see *you* in 1998!" He slurred under his breath, "...Ph'nglui... mglw'nafh Cthulhu... awwww, fuck you, you goddamn cheatin' squid."

Though it was "Bob," I knew who had been the one cheating, for he repeatedly, and not very slickly mind you, yanked cards out of my hand when he claimed he needed them. The whole event, from what little I can remember, was pathetic, but what disturbed me the most was that one of the cards had a picture of our planet on it... and the "alien" looking creature seemed to relish the fact that he had won it.

"Bob," in a panicked state that I had never seen before, hustled me so violently toward the door that we knocked over Mr. Nixon, who was sitting cross-legged on the floor, grilling skewers of meat over an open fire. He cursed us, mumbling that he'd gotten the taste for dog while doing some "brain-massaging" during a trip to North Korea, but now we had ruined his meal, and that we'd all soon be dancing to his tune. Nixon did however hand us a cheaply mimeographed booklet entitled *How To Serve Man*. With that, Mr. Dobbs' face relaxed a little. He nudged me with his elbow, grinning and saying in a bit of an oily voice, "Good recipes in *this* one." He chuckled to himself as we walked out into the misty morning light. I can still hear the dreadful sound and the *import* of his index finger tapping hard against that thin manual of evil.

VI

"WELL, young agent," Mr. Dobbs said to me as we got into his car, "Looks like we have to get you back to Warshington." "Bob" leaned against the large Cadillac and... he actually sighed. I was not sure how to take this turn in his demeanor. Yes, I had been confused and terrified by his actions, but I had yet to see him depressed. It frightened me in a way that I could not previously have imagined. Here stood a man, a *Thing* that exuded all the confidence and power that We as a people not only admire but *need* if we want to survive this complicated abyss that our species has dug for itself. I could only stand still, sick to the stomach, for even though "Bob" is probably insane, he is our best chance, and after witnessing the strangeness and fragile nature of our "powers that be," I could see that no other human savior could redeem our "Slack," as Mr. Dobbs was wont to say. I felt like crying for the first time in years... that is, until Mr. Dobbs stunned me again. He suddenly straightened his back and became hyper alert. My sense of danger ignited as I unconsciously reached for the revolver that I would normally carry in a shoulder holster. Of course it was not there; "Bob" had sold it to some street hood in Miami for a half eaten sandwich. At least that is what he told me.

My eyes darted into the still dim woods around us, fearing the worse, when Mr. Dobbs yelled in a high-pitched voice, "Shiny! Shiny!" and ran to the edge of the dirt parking lot to pick up one small shard of glass among hundreds of shards lying around everywhere. He held it and purred to himself as if he had found a great treasure. His smile returned, full force. I could only simultaneously admire and be disgusted with such a man.

Our drive back to Washington was of course fast and insane. We must have made that drive in record time, for "Bob" never once slowed down; he breezed through traffic lights, stop signs, over hillbillies, and every time a patrol car pulled up behind us with lights flashing, it would either mysteriously lose power and pull off to the side or would suddenly veer off into a direction that "Bob" happened to be looking... sometimes... up... or...down... into the skies or the earth itself! He was still searching for that Skunk Ape.

We stopped only once, and that was to purchase some overripe peaches at a road side stand in Georgia. These peaches "Bob" would throw at specific cars that passed us by. I never figured out the reason, but after he threw one he would bounce up and down in his seat in an exaggerated glee. As much as I would beg him to stop so that I could use a restroom, "Bob" would just scowl at me angrily as if I were asking him to do something horrible. I had to go in my overalls. It did not matter; they stank so badly that no one would have noticed the difference, other than "Bob", who whenever I made a mistake would punch me on the shoulder — damned hard too! — and yell, "I spy with my third nostril... shit" [or "piss" or "weakness"].

It was in a small, rather affluent Virginia town not too far from our Capital that "Bob" deigned to stop at the "safe house" that we employ there. As ashamed as I was to enter and be seen by my colleagues while in such a degraded state, I knew that I had to. I was long overdue, or at least it seemed that way to me. Once we pulled into the driveway, "Bob" graciously opened my door and threw me into the lilac bushes that grow out front, sternly (and frighteningly!) telling me to stay right there, that he had to leave to get some "stuff," adding, "The party isn't over yet by a long shot, Boy." He then "burned rubber" pulling out of the driveway.

My first intention was to run into the safe house and clean myself up, but I feared what "Bob" might do, so I sat in the bushes getting stung in the face by bees while watching various Agents in the house peep through the windows at me in obvious disapproval. I suppose it was then that I realized that I was truly a slave for "Bob." A most horrible feeling. Most horrible indeed.

It was but a few shameful minutes later that "Bob" screeched back into the driveway, carrying a case of cheap beer and a dirty aluminum bucket of what he called "head cheese," even though it looked more like, and smelled more like, rotten fish bait to me. "You beings like this stuff, right?" he asked me. I could only nod my head. "Bob" beckoned me out of the bushes. I stood there before him as he flicked a single mote of dust from my overalls. He then looked me over with a discerning eye and nodded in approval, even though I stank and was filthy.

The key to the house was as always underneath the welcome mat.

I braced myself for all the humiliations that would be heaped upon me, but no one was there to greet me, surprisingly. As if he knew the place, "Bob" led me to the upstairs bedroom where we kept our communications office. Agent X was at the desk, surrounded by a few Agents, and "Bob" banged the bucket of "chum" down in front of him. The pudgy little fuck almost puked. I doubt *he* would have survived a weekend with "Bob!" Mr. Dobbs then grabbed six of the beers from the case, and as he greasily smiled at all of us, proceeded to pull down his trousers and pop the cap off each of the six beers with the power of his buttock muscles alone.

Though I was not astounded, the rest of the "Pinks" (as "Bob" liked to call folks like that) stood aghast in disgust and terror. They all knew the importance of my mission, so when I discretely nodded to them to dig into the bucket of chum and down the "ass beers" (as became Agency History after that day), they did as told like goddamn sheep. Agent X, the chubby useless one, stuttered that there had been an awful tragedy and demanded, "Where in the hell have you been?"

"Bob's" smile disappeared, and in two giant bounds he leaped over to the man, glaring. "Look here, little Pink Boy, I've been gambling with your future and I lost that *and* I lost a pair of gold cufflinks that Connie's sister gave to me. *So what* if one of the clones got damaged?... So what?!... We have plenty more... and if you live long enough, you'll be wishing you had pet rats just so you can eat their shit to survive! So don't whine to *me*, pink boy!" Mr. Dobbs then gave the man a gentle kiss on the forehead and winked at me, whispering, "We don't need no damn agents." I understood. And as he left the house I noticed that somehow, as usual, "Bob" had made off with their wallets.

Mr. Dobbs was incredibly serene, in light of his last outburst of anger, as we drove through the crowed suburban streets and out into the countryside. He seemed to forget everything as fast as it happened, as if he had severe brain damage. He puffed furiously on his pipe, but with that same oblivious grin that he usually wore. I popped a few of his "Pils" that I had left over, just to get rid of the shakes. That, plus the beer I had, made the world seem all that more intense *and* reasonable... It all started to make much more sense than it should, and the drive through the countryside was lovely until "Bob" made a "serious" face again and said, "We'd best lay low until things blow over. I know the place to go, a little inn I have that I like to call Shamalot."

It took us a while to get to this "Shamalot," for Mr. Dobbs seemed constantly to forget where we were driving. He'd stop at random diners, trinket shops, gas stations, etc., where he would feel impelled to make a sale; then we would drive back off in the direction that we had just come from. "Bob" always had *something* in the trunk of his car to sell to these vendors. It was as if he had a second sense for "the sale," and that was what guided him, for wherever we accidentally ended up always seemed to be exactly where he'd originally wanted to go in the first place, but had forgotten about!

We did eventually make it to Shamalot. It was simply an underground type bomb shelter that "Bob" had installed just off the main kitchen of a sprawling hotel complex in rural Virginia. I followed him through the venue; it was a very well appointed hotel, yet the staff seemed lethargic and prone to bumbling and stumbling around. I thought at first that they all might have been overworked or drunk, until I noticed that most of them would shamble off into a dark corner and take a puff off a "smile" pipe every chance they could get. The tobacco they smoked smelled very much like "Bob's", just not as nauseating. We wended our way through this maze until we got to a heavy steel door on which was messily painted, a la *The Little Rascals*, "SHAMALOT, NO PINKS ALOUD!" I recognized "Bob's" childish scrawl and poor spelling. So this, then, would be our safe haven.

VII

SHAMALOT, the place I had expected to look like a typical bomb shelter, was more a mixture of a perverted hip swinger's pad, a communications center of the first order, a hillbilly's hovel, and a museum of oddities. A large stuffed Bigfoot-looking creature stood mounted next to a utilitarian Army surplus metal desk, a bloody scimitar crudely duct taped to its right hand, and at the bottom of the statue, along with a pile of dusty humanoid skulls, was a plaque that stated: *"J.B. "Xlotl" Dobbs XIII: The Beatin' Fist of JHVH-1."* I could not tell you if the thing was once a real beast or not, but its furry body certainly stank like the "frop" that "Bob" always smoked.

As I looked over the shelter/swinger's pad of "Bob's" — mostly to find an alternate escape route — I became aware that we were not alone, for from a far corner came the sound of shallow rasping breaths. Even after all the events that I had witnessed, I still held some fear of the unknown in my heart. With trepidation I slowly walked to the corner from which the sounds emanated. There, in an easy chair, illuminated by the dim and wavy light of a Lava Lamp, sat a grotesque version of what once was probably human. Its face was a sickening parody. It had a permanent sardonic grin and between its strained lips was a poorly grafted-on pipe much like "Bob's". The man-thing exuded a continuous soft and disgusting chuckle that sounded like the sarcasm of the damned. I found myself backing away, but with a withered hand the creature beckoned me to it. "Hehehe," it chuckled. "Have I got a joke for you!" The thing then proceeded to tell a long, rambling and incoherent "joke" about a priest, a Pink and a Yeti that go to some bar. It made no sense whatsoever, yet the creature kept laughing to itself as it puffed on its pipe.

I did not even notice that "Bob" had approached and was standing next to me, until he let out a room-shaking guffaw at what I suppose was the punch line *"Humanity popping like a bunch of goddamn crawfish in a hot skillet."* I shook my head in disgust and told this thing before me, "Shut the hell up! We may be on the brink of atomic war!" Mr. Dobbs twisted my ear in a most painful manner and, while patting the thing on its shoulder, said "*Fuck* 'em if they can't take a joke."

Suddenly a very real and cold fear gripped my heart. I asked "Bob" if he knew something I didn't. Did Khrushchev die of alcohol poisoning? Did the Commies assassinate our President in retaliation? Were we on the brink of atomic destruction?

"Bob" just "played pocket pool" and chuckled, "Nuclear war is the least of your worries, young Agent, especially after last night's card game." It was then that the room suddenly lit up in red lights and a Klaxon started to sound. "Bob" jumped up and down like a child on Christmas day, yelling, "That's Connie calling! That's Connie calling!" He skipped (I am not kidding) over to a Video-Telephonic Device. There he sat down, fidgeting on a large leather swivel chair, still furiously playing pocket pool.

"Hi Sweetie Spleen!" He said to the beautiful image of Connie on the video screen. "What are you doing in our Dallas compound?" Mr. Dobbs smiled stupidly as Connie said, "Well, Deary, I had a little party at the compound last and, and, uh, well, it would seem that I made a little joke with Jackie about pranking the President... you know what a card he is... and it would seem that three of the Doktors overheard." Mr. Dobbs just nodded his head, smiling as if he could picture the party in his "mind." "Well, this morning those Doktors got all drunked up and took some rifles... and, well, Deary, it would seem that Doktor Oswald was a tad bit too tipsy and grabbed some real bullets instead of the rubber kind." Connie made a gesture, and on the video screen Dr. Oswald appeared sitting next to her, looking sheepish and more than a bit hung over. "Sorry, "Bob,"" he said with a hang-dog expression on his face, obviously twisting his foot on the floor in shame. Connie popped a Pil in his mouth as a reward, which he gobbled down like an obedient dog.

"Its okay, Dr. Oswald," "Bob" said. "We all make mistakes. 'Fuck up... man up... man, shut the fuck up.' It's our motto, isn't it?" I was shocked again at "Bob's" levity in situations of danger. "Well... fuck ...us... if... we... can't take a joke!" "Bob" elbowed me so hard in the ribs that I fell over gasping. "Have Connie give you a few more Pils and fifty cents to go see a movie, Lee. I'll call Johnny Boy and clear the whole thing up." Dr. Oswald nodded obediently and walked away from the screen, grinning like a reprieved man, chewing a big mouthful of Pils.

"Look, Connie," "Bob" said, "Where is Dr. Ruby?"

"He and the other Doktors are down at his strip joint keeping the party going," Connie replied, looking as radiant as ever.

"Well, do me a favor, Honey Bunch of Synapses, and go down there and tell Dr. Ruby that I have a job for him. I want him to take Doktor Oswald out." "Bob" said.

"Will Do!" Connie chirped as they both jiggled their fingers at their throats, making a bizarre noise, and hung up their video-phones.

"Bob" then looked strangely thoughtful for a moment, "I guess I should have told Connie that the job was to get Dr. Oswald out of the country... for a little bit... hmmmm." He then pulled out a folder full of photos from the desk drawer, and began to meticulously cut and paste Dr. Oswald's head onto various figures: railroad conductors, nurses, dinosaurs, and photos of men holding rifles with crudely painted signs that said "I DID IT!" He sighed a lot during the process, until the sighs became a sort of barking noise, guttural and animalistic. He stood up and smoothed some non-existent wrinkles from his trousers, right before he pulled them down and sat on a nearby portable chemical toilet. I averted my eyes until "Bob" yelled *GAZE UPON ME, LITTLE PINK!* I actually stumbled backwards at the timbre of his voice, yet I found myself obeying his command as I dragged a metal folding chair over to him and sat down within a few mere inches of him as he did his business — which in itself was odd, for as I gazed upon his face, it turned rather vividly from green to red to blue and back to green again until, with the sound of a million balloons popping simultaneously, what had previously been a very serious, strained look on his face transformed into the usual moronic and placid visage that I not only would see in person, but henceforth in my own mind as well when I closed my eyes. I suspect that I was going insane from all the PILS and "Slack." One could only guess.

My feeling of insanity was pretty much cemented when "Bob" picked up a girlie pink video-phone and called our *still living* President! It would appear that the S.O.B. was a dipsomaniac, a whore-monger and still at the bordello in Florida.

A Gray with a powder blue bouffant wig came up on screen

looking annoyed and drunk, its huge eyes clouded over. It appeared to be in a bed, as it rolled over and got the President on phone. Our President rubbed his red rimmed eyes and in an irritated, stuttering voice asked first if Jackie were there. When soothingly reassured by "Bob" that she was back in Dallas, he calmed down a bit until he was told of all that had transpired in his besotted absence. The President jumped out of bed. He was clothed in a _____ uniform! I lost ALL respect for him at that point, but could only admire his obvious abilities, as M_____ M_____ and the bouffanted Gray kept adjusting an eye patch, which, it would seem, covered the eye damage that M_____ M_____ had done the night before with a fork. I listened in as the two of them conversed.

"Bob" kept trying to explain to the whining man that "it's all right" and that "he [I am not sure who he meant] didn't have to worry because I have it all under control." The President threw another fit while "Bob" explained to him that his trusted man, Doktor Oswald, was the one who had drunkenly grabbed the rifle with the real bullets. The President suggested that they dispose of the assassinated clone, and he himself could explain on T.V. that he was all right and that any injury was "just a scratch." "Bob" snickered, saying, "It's a grand idea but obviously, no eye patch is going fool the necessary amount of people when thousands saw half your head being blown off. So just accept the Island offer and shut up."

"Bob" rocked back in his swivel chair, a smug look on his face, as if he had just untied The Gordian Knot. He played "pocket pool" so hard that I could hear the sound of *pain*. The President glowered thoughtfully for a moment, taking in the import of the situation he had found himself in.

"Okay, Master" the President said. "I'll take the deal. Just tell Jackie that I am getting stuff done with the Grays at Canaveral, and send Doktor Oswald to me. I have a few choice fists to show him." Mr. Dobbs chucked and mentioned that he already had Doktor Ruby on the job. "He is gonna take him out of the country." "Bob" then abruptly hung up the phone, "Did I tell Connie the 'out of the country' part?" He looked serious for a few moments until the Thing in the easy chair started laughing insanely, yelling, "When "Bob" done fucks up, people die! When Mr. Dobbs starts fartin' the world starts... hehehehehe." I glared at the creature in disgust, demanding, "How can you joke at this moment?" I whispered an aside to "Bob," asking what manner of foul creature it was that sat in the corner. Ignoring my attempt at privacy "Bob" said loudly, pointing to the creature and laughing, "Hehehe... *that* is a *mistake*! A genetic mistake like the Alligator People that you saw in my Grand Moat of Happiness outside the factory. That *mistake* used to be as Pink as you... it *was* my Middle Hand Man, until IT decided to retire to a Monastery in Tibet with a big bag of MY personal stash of Frop. The *thing* we got back from the Yeti Monks was no long human, but also not quite an OverMan... so I decided to graft that pipe onto its face and *make* it frop up twenty-four hours a day to see what would happen. Young Agent, what you see before you is the Future of Failure. What you see is an OverUnderMan." The thing in the corner puffed its pipe and cackled like a madman.

"You see, Young Agent," "Bob" told me, "That I now need *you* as my Middle Hand Man."

I pondered the gravity of what he had told me as he put some atonal "rumba" music on the hifi and went to the classy bar to fix us a drink. He did a poor job of hiding the spiking of my drink with Pils, though he obviously tried to look innocent and hide his actions. My heart dropped as he started to subtly gyrate his hips, hula-style, when he glided over with my drink. We were alone, and I had no escape. I feared the worst but knew that this was my duty. "Bob" handed me the drink and suddenly got serious, if you can ever call him that. He heartily "pwhiffed" the stuffy air that hung leaden in the shelter. He told me not to worry too much, that he'd find a way to "make a buck out of the whole thing." Without thinking, I drank the cocktail down. The room spun in pleasant way and I noticed that the little umbrella that he had put into the drink was topped off with a small plastic bobbily head of the President. The head had what *looked* like *two bullet holes* in it. I knew then that God help us if we cannot get this man "Bob" squarely on our side.

"Bob" gyrated around me while my sight dimmed into a fearful tunnel and my mind reeled at the import of this man's powers. "Bob" stood over me as I slumped in the chair. "Boy, I have plans for you. You're going to Dobbstown for further instruction — and a little itty-bitty operation to open that *other* hole." I felt the room whirl as all faded out but his pipe, his grin and that insufferable soft chuckling.

THE END

?

The Agent
Goes to
Dobbstown

Prologue

The Package

IN August of 2007 I was awakened early one morning by the doorbell. When I answered the door I saw (and smelled) before me a wino. Although he had an immaculate haircut, he was quite obviously a bum. No one in my neighborhood wore ripped sweat pants, a dirty parka and mismatched sneakers on a hot and humid summer morning. Of course, the bottle of Mad Dog "wine" sticking out of his pocket was itself a dead give away. Sure, we all enjoy indulging in the Dog every once in a while, but by the smell of this fellow, he must have already consumed enough of it to almost mask his unwashed aroma. I was not too sure of what to do at first. His eyes were downcast and he was mumbling to himself words that I could not quite make out. I reached for the change and key jar that I kept by the door, intending on giving him some cash and to get myself back to bed, when he suddenly thrust a dirty manila envelope toward me. "The guy with wings told me to give this to you."

I took the envelope despite its filth. The wino yet stood at my door with his eyes downcast. I sensed fear emanating from him — or was it relief? Groggy and not sure what to do, I thanked him. I was finally beginning to understand what really was transpiring. I knew, albeit with dread, that I would have to get to work on this project ASAP.

As I began to close the screen door the bum shoved in a dirty (and much too large for him) red sneaker to block me. I looked closer at his face. There were traces of white clown paint around his chin and forehead, and his nose, which I thought red from alcoholism, was actually red from paint only partially rubbed off. "Spare some change, Chump?" he asked me. I grabbed a fistful of coins and deposited them into his outstretched hand. "Spare some frop, man?" he asked in return. I told him I had stopped fropping years ago. Unabashed he asked, "How 'bout some of them good Pils then, buddy?" I told him I was all out as I pushed his foot out of the way and unceremoniously closed and locked the door in his face.

My heart started to beat faster and a panic rose in me as I trotted to my desk. I tossed the heavy envelope down and knowing this was going to be a time-consuming and probably illusion-shattering assignment. I took a deep breath and looked out the back window, hoping that this was all a dream. But all I saw was the same wino, squatting pants-down in my back yard, taking a dump while he leered up at me. I knew then that this job was going to really suck. *They* don't send a used-up, worn out Bozo to deliver good assignments. But it was now in my hands, a done deal.

The following is *not* something that I wish to reveal; in fact at the risk of my safety I have blacked out many of the revelations — some for national security, others because the information revealed is simply too terrible for the world at large to know.

Top half of page blacked out up to this point.

...was late afternoon when I finally woke up. I was still very hazy, befuddled really. "Bob" was driving us in a rickety old pickup truck rather too fast down a bumpy country road. I could tell we were in the deep South from the aroma that hung in the humid air, the red soil that lined the sides of the median, and the program that was blaring on the car radio — a crazed-sounding preacher ranting about something or other in a Southern patois so heavy that I could barely understand what he was saying. "Bob" seemed to be listening intently, giggling at the more serious bits about "hellfire" and shaking his head in disgust at the more contemporary bits. But for the most part it was giggling, and after Mr. Dobbs noticed I was awake, he shot a few incongruous asides to me in regards to what the preacher was saying. He seemed to take it as a scripted comedy radio program. After a few minutes "Bob" shook his head and turned off the radio, telling me, "They just don't make 'em like they used to anymore. The script writers just aren't as inspired *as scared*, ho-hum."

I asked "Bob" where we were and where we were heading. He of course ignored me, but did grab a bottle of peach soda from an aluminum cooler that sat between us. He stuck the top of the bottle in his ear and gave it a jerk, prying off the cap before handing me the bottle. The cap stayed lodged in his ear. "Bob" didn't seem to notice, or didn't mind. The soda was ice cold and refreshing. As hot as it was, and as thirsty as I was, I drank it in one gulp. (Imagine the worst hangover and multiply that by a factor of ten.) When I asked "Bob" if he had more of the drink, he just smiled, told me "Sodee-pop is bad for the feet," and continued to drive.

I could tell that we were heading in a westerly direction because of the setting sun, but I was still not sure exactly where we were, not even the state we were in, until we drove through the crossing of a more substantial road where a sign indicated that we were in Arkansas heading toward a town called Lewisville. It still didn't allow me to know our destination, but I did feel a bit more secure knowing where I was.

We had been driving for maybe half an hour when "Bob" removed a worn velvet tobacco pouch from his pocket. His face took on a rare grimace as he filled his pipe with the last "shake" of his frop — just a pinch, really. However, once he lit up his pipe, his face again relaxed.

This happy, unconcerned "Bob" didn't last long, for once the frop was all burned up, "Bob's" mood again changed. He no longer drove casually, with his attention mostly *off* the task of driving. He now drove in a rigid and tense manner, his eyes sternly on the road and his hands gripping the steering wheel so tightly that I thought its Bakelite might shatter. Although "Bob's" driving had slowed markedly, he now seemed to hit every bump and pothole in the road. This just added to my discomfort and to "Bob's" increasingly dark mood. Every once in a while he would stop the truck, stick his head out the open window, and take deep nostrils-full of the Southern air. His eyes would half close in a sort of squint and follow as best he could some scent that only he detected.

We had gone some few miles on a very rough dirt road, more of a path really, when we hit a deep pothole. The jarring and the carbonated drink I had imbibed earlier caused me to let out a rather loud belch. "Bob" slammed on the brakes and my head flew forward, hitting the dash. I shook off the pain and looked to "Bob." He was glaring at me now with such anger that I was taken aback. I pardoned myself, hoping that would defuse his anger. Instead he bared his teeth and growled, "Your human smells disgust me!"

I again apologized for my indiscretion, but that seemed only to agitate "Bob" further.

He began to shake, and yelled quite loudly at me, "I want YOUR Slack!" With that he lifted his right leg and, with eyes rolled to the back of his head, he let out a most tremendous belch and fart at the same time. It literally shook the truck and set my ears to buzzing. I pushed myself to the far end of the seat, expecting a most foul odor. Luckily his emanations smelled oddly of maple and vanilla. "Bob" did seem a bit more relaxed after this release, though his agitation and dark mood continued.

As we drove further into the wilds of rutted Arkansas back roads, "Bob" started to sniff the air more intensely. The sun was now setting; however, I did not fear getting lost, for my experiences with "Bob" led me to trust in his dumb luck.

It was in the gloaming when "Bob" pulled off the road next to a marshy area. He bade me to get out and follow him; that I did. About twenty yards into the marshy woods "Bob" stopped me with a hand to my shoulder. He took a few deep breaths and let out a scream, an animal-like call. "WRREEE! WREET! WRRRREEEE!" It sounded much like a farmer calling to his pigs. We then stood silent as he sniffed the air and cocked an ear to the deep woods. A smile came back to his face as a distant returning call was heard. "Bob" repeated his cry once again, and we received one in return. Within minutes I could see the outline of a hulking figure coming toward us. To be quite honest I was frightened; my anus clenched tightly. The last time I had an encounter with one of these beasts... well, let's just say I don't like to think about it.

This creature, which I can only describe as a more yellowish brown version of the "Swamp Ape" I had unfortunately met in Florida, approached us. He — believe me, it was a he — was looking me up and down with a leering eye that I feared. It was clear now what "Bob" wanted, and why he had been so agitated earlier. "Bob" needed his frop!

The creature, which "Bob" referred to as Dan or "Boggy Creek Dan," led us down a narrow path in the woods. "Bob" and the creature were conversing in a strange language, with the creature leering back at me every few words. I of course was very uncomfortable at the prospects, but I had a duty to perform for my nation and would unhappily fulfill that duty, be what may.

We finally came to what I can only describe as an outdoor latrine in a small glade in the woods. There were huge piles of Boggy Creek Dan feces dotting the ground, and in each pile there grew a tall greenish weed. The stench was near unbearable as the two looked over each plant, with "Dan" often gesturing at me. The damned beast had an erection. I love my nation! — but sometimes I think I go to far for it. Luckily for me, "Bob" drew an empty soda bottle from his pocket and handed it to the beast, who seemed quite pleased with the exchange and wandered off into the woods rubbing the bottle on his erection. "Bob" giggled as he stuffed his pipe and tobacco pouch full of buds from the frop plants. Much more relaxed now, "Bob" started to chat on the walk back to the truck, telling me that Dan was an all right sort, none too bright but "always good for the frop."

We drove on in the now pitch-dark night. As I suspected, "Bob" had no problem finding the way back to a main route. He again grew "chatty" once we got back on the road, babbling on about God knows what, though I am sure it made sense to him. After a while he drew a miniature version of his pipe out of the glove compartment and filled it full of frop. This he handed to me and then lit it up with a battered Zippo lighter. The taste and stench of the frop was horrific, but soon I started to relax. Everything seemed strange, out of place, but I found that I was no longer worrying as much about my near future as I had been before. I felt that everything would just turn out for the best. I can certainly see why "Bob" constantly smokes this stuff. And his babbling started to make some sense to me, too! Our top scientists need to look into this "frop" thing for good or for ill.

My thoughts and perceptions were beginning to really play some havoc on me after the second pipefull. Things get a bit hazy from here, but while I was staring out the window observing nature pass by me and listening to "Bob's" soothing voice, the truck struck something heavy in the road. Mr. Dobbs duly pulled over. In the pitch dark it was hard to see what we had hit, but there was a light shining in a ditch nearby. "Bob" and I walked over to it. The light was coming from an old-fashioned railroad lantern, and next to it lay a headless man in dirty overalls. I let out a worried sigh, believing we had just killed a man. "Bob," on the other hand, chuckled to himself as he squatted down and lifted the man up by the torso. It may be the frop, but this headless man stood on his own! Indeed when "Bob" reached down, picked up the lantern and placed it in the headless man's left hand, the man grasped it tightly! Mr. Dobbs then proceeded to say "Sorry" and patted the stump of the man's neck, who in turn started to wriggle his back side around just as a happy dog would. I could only but stare at this, when the events got stranger still! The headless man took a greasy fifty-dollar bill out of his pocket and handed it to "Bob," I guessed as a form of thanks for giving him his lantern back. "Bob" smiled and said, "Thanks Casey. Good luck finding your head."

Back in the truck it took me a few minutes to get my voice. I said to "Bob," "I've seen some very strange things in my times with you, but this is just impossible! You just decapitated a man with your truck and not only is he still standing and walking around, but he gave you fifty dollars! What the hell is going on?"

"Bob" turned to me with his trademark smile. "Look here, Mister G-Man, that there was Ol' Casey. He got his head chopped off in a hilariously tragic train accident some years back, and he's been looking for his head ever since. I know where it is, but it is just too funny to run into him every once in a while, and anyway he is always good for the exact amount of cash I need. That fifty he gave me is just what we need to get a present for a very special friend of mine. You'll meet him."

With that he snickered to himself, mumbling under his breath that I would "see stranger still." To calm my still jumpy nerves, "Bob" passed me a handful of Pils. I knew what mind-altering damage they could do, but with all the frop in my system I decided it could really get no worse. I thought I was losing my mind anyway. With the Pils, "Bob" gave me another peach soda with the warning, "You can fart all you want... but no belching, Human."

The Pils had taken full effect by the time we hit Texarkana. I was up, down and sideways. I wasn't even sure if I could walk when "Bob" pulled over at a sort of Souvenir-Trinket-Lunch Counter-Gas Station. The inside was much too bright for my eyes; it looked uncannily like a poor quality television program playing before me. Mr. Dobbs walked right up to the counter and talked to a surly looking man standing behind it. "Bob" was pointing at a war surplus Italian Carcano carbine with a scope that was mounted on the wall. A sign above it said, in small print, "Just like," and in large print "The Rifle That Assassinated President Kennedy." Mr. Dobbs handed the man the fifty dollar bill. The man handed him the rifle. We got back into the truck.

"*Attempted* assassination." "Bob" chuckled to himself as we drove on deeper into Texas.

I asked him what our destination was. He replied "Someplace," and followed that up with "... But we are going to Texas for now." I thought that was quite obvious as I drifted off into a drug-induced sleep with the soft voice of "Bob" droning in the background about monsters, UFOs and the stock market.

II

I woke up late the next afternoon in the back seat of a brand new Cadillac DeVille convertible. Luckily for me it was a convertible, for when a young man banged on the window and yelled "Drop your socks and grab your cocks!" I was startled enough that my military training kicked in, and I sat straight up fast enough to have knocked my head on the roof of a normal car.

In a firm but quieter tone the man told me, ""Bob" wants to see you, Mister G-Man, so hurry it on up."

I exited the car rubbing my eyes, confused as to how I had ended up in a Cadillac car when last I remembered, "Bob" and I were in an old Ford pickup truck. I asked the young fellow where we were and how I'd ended up in the Cadillac. It was all a blur to me. The frop and Pils hangover was not too bad, but the night before seemed distant and fuzzy.

"Yeah," the young man said to me with a slight South African accent. ""Bob" told me this morning that outside Dallas late last night, he ran into a traveling, *ahem*, Woman's Health and Comfort Devices salesman, and convinced him to trade his old pickup for the new caddy, explaining to the Yank that folks in these parts would trust him more if he drove a beat-up truck. Man, "Bob" can sell a shit you just took right back to you, and he'd be right too. I should know, that's how I met him. Long story though."

We both leaned against the car as I yawned and got my bearings. In front of me was a modern rambling ranch house surrounded by a squares of well-tended lawn, the late afternoon sun making everything look a little washed out... or maybe that was the frop still in my system. I took a deep breath and stretched. We started toward the front door but the young man stopped me.

"Seriously, roll down your socks and grab your dick... house rules."

I looked him up and down. I could see his socks peeking from under his cuffed jeans; they were rolled down, and he did have his right hand on his crotch. He also, for some reason, had his left hand grabbing a bulge just above his left knee. I duly rolled down my socks and cupped my crotch. We walked in this awkward way to the front door. The young man didn't bother knocking on the door, he just opened it up and we walked right in.

The change of atmosphere was welcome. Not only was the air conditioning refreshing, but the house looked "normal," quite well appointed and modern. We walked through the wide vestibule to a large kitchen where the smell of frying food brought more relief, for I was very hungry by this time. Standing next to the steaming stove stood a woman clad only in an apron. It could only be Connie Dobbs; one cannot forget such a lovely rear end. However, just above her tail bone there flicked back and forth a monkey's tail. Judging by the redness around the base of the tail, it would seem that she recently had gotten it grafted on, for what purpose I never asked.

The young man gave a small cough to get Connie's attention. When Connie turned around she immediately recognized me. She put down the spatula she was using and gave me a hug, one hand squeezing my buttocks and her tail pushing away my hand that cupped my crotch. The other hand, sadly, was checking for a nonexistent wallet in my front pocket, but "Bob" of course had taken that earlier. Still, I didn't mind. Connie's presence was enough to satisfy any man or woman, or, judging from my last experience with her, gray-skinned non-humanoids.

Our reunion was interrupted by "Bob," who walked into the kitchen exclaiming in a very loud and happy voice, "By Wotan, Connie, that frying prairie squid sure smells great!"

Connie, a bit annoyed, replied, "GGG hunted it down fresh this morning. You would have known if you hadn't been messing with *that* all morning."

She pointed at his torso. I was taken a bit aback. He was entirely nude, but that was not what disturbed me. It was what he was doing. "Bob" was standing in front of us thrusting his penis into the neck of a severed head. If that wasn't bad enough, I noticed that with every thrust the head groaned, and its eyes rolled back... and, on the whites of the eyes, Mr. Dobbs had evidently scrawled dollar signs in black ink. He just stood there smiling at us, thrusting away, emitting low moans. He began to shiver and with a mighty thrust he yelled out, "Serendipity!" The head groaned and "Bob" shuddered.

He removed the head from his manhood and set it on the counter, much to Connie's disgust. She rolled her eyes, saying, "Looks like GGG and the whole state of 'Missourah' will be my companions tonight."

The young man who had woken me that afternoon smiled broadly and said, "You bet your sweet monkey tail I'll do you right, Connie!"

"Bob" laughed, turned to me and pointed to the head. "See, I told you that I knew where Ol' Casey's head was." He sighed, looking a little forlorn. "Suppose he won't want that back now. Anyway, welcome to Dobbs Ranch. I'd like your help rounding up some stray cattle today."

With that Mr. Dobbs walked around the counter and gave Connie a quick peck on the cheek and a rather lurid tail rub. He then retrieved from a corner a long package wrapped in newspaper comics pages.

Looking at us he said, "I see you've met Gillian Gordon Gordon. He's a fine young chap. I got him on loan from the Air Force. Constance said that this very morning he hunted down the prairie squid we'll be having for dinner tonight."

Turning to the young man he said, "Bet you would have gotten more with this."

He handed the package to who I now guessed was called GGG. The young man opened it up. It was the Italian carbine that "Bob" had purchased in Texarkana along with a few clips of ammunition.

"I sure would have, "Bob,"" he said, cycling the rifle bolt and pointing it out the window. "Hell, I had to grab the slimy little buggers by hand and gnaw off their heads. And what is more, had I been in Dallas back in '63 with this I could have gotten three rounds into the Kennedy clone, *and* three into that inept idiot of a Doktor, Oswald, all in under 5.6 seconds." He turned to me. "And Mister G-Man, never call me Gillian! It's GGG or else..." He cycled the bolt again and stared at me. He was serious, but I had commanded men like him in Korea. I could see he was made of good stuff and I was later proved right. This rather tall, handsome and lanky young man called GGG would save my life more than once in the months to come.

"Bob" gave a nod of approval, but of course, with him, one is never sure exactly of what he approving, disapproving, thinking or even doing. In fact at most times I am not sure if he is even aware of his surroundings or even what he himself is thinking.

Mr. Dobbs cracked his knuckles, his neck and then somehow his penis. He let out a "hrumph" sound and, pointing to a door off the kitchen, said to me, "Young Agent, go in there and take a shower. Pee-yeww, you stink. There's a change of clothing for you on the bed. Make it snappy, we have work to do."

I nodded my assent. "OK, Mr. Dobbs, will do." I then went off for one of the last showers I would have in a long time.

Rest of document (75 pages) blanked out.

I

THE sensation of movement stirred me to consciousness, but it was the lush, feral odors of a Southern pine forest rushing by my nostrils that truly woke me from my stupor. I unglued my Pils-glazed eyelids and found the bright headlights of "Bob's" Cadillac bouncing wildly off of the green foliage of frighteningly tall and grotesque pines as we sped down a lonely red dirt side road, somewhere in the South. Oddly, the little specks of dust in the headlight beams looked like miniature faces of "Bob": "Dobbsheads," as I had begun to call them. When I looked to my side, sure enough, "Bob" was gleaming at me from the driver's seat, not driving, mind you, but grinning at me while he picked his nose, his finger going so far up his nostril that one of his eyes bulged out.

"Can't get that damn Irish Spring smell of the Pinks outta my nose. And this here is *prime* Boggy Creek Monster territory! But if I can't smell 'em then I can't milk 'em!" He paused, his finger still up his nose, while his grin waxed sleazier. "These Arkansas Yeti smell to high heaven, but *damn*," he yelled, punching the steering wheel. "They sure do love a good wrassle, and their Sex Gland secretes the most *potent* aphrodisiac known to Yetikind. And let me tell you, son... you ever fuck an elephant? Well, no pachyderm will deny you that pleasure, once you put a little Boggy Creek Monster juice behind your ears! Yiiiiiii,Yiiiiii!!!!" He screamed so loud that I had to cover my ears.

This nightmare, I now realized, was not over by a long shot. That fact became all too obvious when Mr. Dobbs shoved a piece of paper under my nose saying, "Smell upon this, boy! Go ahead, *PWIFF* it!" My trembling hands — probably the D.T.s — took the paper and "pwhiffed" it. I must admit it smelled clean, new, real, like ozone... and NOT of this earth. "That, boy," he went on, "is the *pstench* of your freedom!" I looked over the paper and sure enough, the Agency had *sold* me, *legally*, to Mr. Dobbs. It was all in the contract, and it was definitely legal. My heart sank.

Then in the bat of an eye "Bob" slammed on the brakes so hard that we did many wild 360's on the slick dirt road, my head hitting the dash board, breaking open the many recently healed head wounds I had gotten in my travails with "Bob." He laughed, bleating over and over, "Bleeding Head good! Healed Head bad!" while bouncing up and down in his seat, until I started to scream hysterically out of pain and general frustration. "Bob" must have found this funny, for he matched my screams *exactly* but to a much higher pitch and decibel than is humanly possible. He then grabbed my shoulders, stared painfully deeply into my eyes and shook the hell out of me. "You can *smell* it, boy! You can *smell* it, boy!" he screamed as the car slid off the road and into a water-filled ditch.

"Damn! There's a stinky one around here!" Mr. Dobbs then, with superhuman strength, pulled me bodily out of my seat and ran into the marshy woods with me over his shoulder as if I were as light as a rag doll. He must have carried me half a mile deep into the brooding woods when just as suddenly he flung me, hard, to the muddy ground. "Now keep your *pstench* quiet, boy, one of them Ol' Boggys is around here somewhere." I quietly pulled myself up from the mud, pleased that I still had the old hillbilly's overalls on; at least "Bob" had let me keep them.

Mr. Dobbs laid his cold hand solidly on my shoulder, while in much too loud voice he whispered, "Shhhh, the fine beast is behind those trees... they're a tricky breed, these ones... they'll try to fool you, try to lull you into a Frop-Slack just before they pounce on you. Keep still and for the love of Patecatl, keep your damned pinkish *pstench* down!"

Just then the thick brush in front of us parted, and through it came the foulest smelling eight foot tall hairy man-beast. It had its eyes cast to the ground but had a moronic, unmistakably Dobbs-like grin on its face — a grin I just knew meant trouble. In its mud-matted red-furred hand was a bouquet of wilted wild flowers! These it held out to Mr. Dobbs in a submissive manner.

"Bob" took two confident strides up to the creature, took the flowers, flung them first over his shoulder, and then, in the swiftest martial arts move I had ever seen, tossed the beast onto its belly. Mr. Dobbs had the animal good and cold then and there but he let it get up in its fury. "Bob" winked at me, saying in an aside "I like a good monster wrassle too, son."

They then got into a low down and dirty "wrasslin' match" of Biblical proportions. The woods shook with thuds and grunts that rumbled in the pit of my stomach. By God, they were *enjoying* themselves! — that is, until "Bob" finally pinned the beast down and forced its rear end into the air. He flippantly tossed me a small vial and commanded me, "Get that fine ambrosia! The gland is in their ass!" I did as told. The gland was not actually located in the beast's anus, but too close to it for my comfort. I was glad at that moment that "Bob" hadn't fed me in a while. Once the animal was "milked," Mr. Dobbs pulled out a hunk of *humanoid* jerky from his jacket pocket and handed it to the beast. The two then sat down on a big rotting log, smoked their pipes and conversed in a language that I did not understand but that sounded a bit like an ancient version of the Sino-Tibetan Mother tongue.

I was in a bad way from delirium tremens, stress, fear, exhaustion and all. The events I had experienced recently had frayed my soul to its bare threads. I needed, I shamefully admit, some more of "Bob's" Pils just to get my *other* mind together, as "Bob" might say when he puffed on his pipe.

I gathered up my courage to interrupt the two, and asked him — too meekly, probably, for "Bob" hated meekness — for some of them Pils. With a deft flick of his thumb, "Bob" tossed one-way off course! However, at that exact moment I happened to faint and keel over into the mud, quite coincidentally into exactly the perfect position for the errant Pil, and some swamp water, to *just happen* to pop into my mouth. I immediately felt better. Once again things started to make sense.

I sat down next to "Bob" and the monster, and somehow was able to join in the conversation. I know that I simply babbled, trying to sound like Them, but somehow They understood what I was saying — although they seemed to laugh heartily at some grammatical mistakes of mine. "Bob" put his hand, gently this time, on my shoulder, saying, "You owe me a favor, young Agent, and after that, let's get you to Dobbstown for some proper language lessons."

I will never tell *what* he made me do with that Arkansas Skunk Ape. To this day, even though I am "tight like a dollar" with "Bob," I shall never forgive him for that... that perversion of nature that I had to tithe him.

II

M R. Dobbs did not take me directly to Dobbstown as he had promised, which was a good thing in retrospect. Instead he insisted in his own easy manner that he needed to make a quick stop in Dallas to "... Oh, you know, just to pick up a few things, bop Connie, make a deal or two, have a little chat with that Doktor Oswald, eviscerate a couple of cows, and see how this vial of semi-liquid Looove works on a herd of Prairie Squid." Mr. Dobbs suddenly thrust that accursed vial under my nose, his grin looking rather menacing, almost a sneer. I squirmed away to the far passenger corner of the front seat and curled into a fetal position, cowering and shaking.

Just thinking about what it took to fill that horrid vial, and the price I had to pay to be "Bob's" "boy," was more painful than most humans could imagine. As I shut my eyes tight, holding back the tears and the shame, his demonic chuckle swished around my ears, and yet no matter how tightly shut I held my eyes, all I could see was a terrifying myriad of disembodied Dobbsheads floating within my minds eye. I was about to burst into full blown insanity when something told me to look at *him*.

There his face was, inches away from mine, still attached to his body. His grin once again seemed benign, albeit semi-retarded. The malevolent *thing* that was moments ago tormenting me now imbued me with a strange hope, *an inspiration*, or maybe it was just the Pil "Bob" popped into my awe-opened mouth.

The rest of the ride to Dallas went well enough. Mr. Dobbs told bad joke after bad joke, but the way he told them made me laugh. (Pils, maybe.) He also filled me in as to what I might expect at Dobbstown. Although it would be no piece of cake, he told me, I would get extensive training in languages, *real* politics, astrophysics, and, oddly, Modern Science Fiction Cinema.

The closer we got to Dallas the calmer "Bob" became, until he stopped talking altogether but beamed in an almost beatific way. This struck me as a bit odd, for he still had to deal with the fallout from his Doktors' drunken assassination prank. However, I begun to accept that trying to understand "Bob" was a big, *big*, mistake, and that just letting "Bob" be "Bob" — observing him, un-listening to him and not taking anything seriously around him — was one's best bet at getting through the whole Dobbs experience in one piece, spiritually and physically. It was obvious to me at the time too that I had much to learn.

We finally made it to the Dobbs compound outside of Dallas. It was a real compound, complete with high and thick brick walls, guard posts, and of course a moat, albeit this time filled with actual alligators. When I expressed confusion as to why it was outside of Dallas, a city about which he talked quite a lot, he just continued beaming and muttered something about "those damn Death Ray ordinances."

The guards at the massive wrought-iron gates looked just like "Bob's" agents that had picked me up on the first fateful (fatal?) day a few weeks back. They even had that same spaced-out, fropped-up look, and they too still smelled to high heaven.

Once safely inside the compound, Mr. Dobbs let out a preternaturally long and deep sigh, his eyes rolling to the back of his head (literally) as he crashed the Cadillac into the back of his five car garage. I noted, before my forehead smashed on the dashboard once again, that he had run over a man pointing a gun in our direction.

"Bob" recovered from his ecstasy as he got out of the car, and I spilled out of my side. He approached the body of the would-be assassin, stooped over, pulled the man's wallet from his pocket, extracted the cash from it, and said, in an almost sad sounding voice, "Hmmmm... thought I could trust that guy. Oh well... ready for some lunch, young Agent?" I could only nod in approval as "Bob" tossed the wallet over his shoulder. The wallet somehow fell back into the dead man's rear pocket, which was strange, for he was still lying on his back. This Mr. Dobbs has some amazing tricks... or are they Powers?

We entered his stately mansion. This one looked ready for war: all reinforced concrete, machine gun ports, and of course signs everywhere, in Dobbs' childish scrawl, saying: "Keep Out!!!" No servant bothered to offer me a bandage for my heavily bleeding wound, but Connie did meet us in the cavernous front entrance with a tray holding three martinis, a plate of finely sliced monkey brains suspended in a sort of neon green Jello, and a sympathy note for "Bob" from Doktor Ruby. "Bob" rather uncouthly downed all the contents of the silver tray, note included, in a matter of seconds. His frop-dulled eyes brightened as he reached down his own throat and pulled up a monkey-brains-stained piece of paper from his gullet. He read it to himself as he softly hummed. "So it appears that Doktor Ruby feels bad about the prank he pulled on Doktor Oswald... well, it's no skin off my nose, 'cause today I just found out that my Bobco Conspiracy, UFOs N' Stuff book publishing company had its stock shoot through the roof! I guess that's a small price to pay for the loss of one clone... and anyway, that Kennedy was getting on my nerves. Couldn't exsanguinate a damn cow in under fifteen minutes and leave it with a smile on its face, if his life depended on it. However, that Jackie! Oooh LaLa!" Mr. Dobbs proceeded to run over to the doorway and violently hump the lintel, squealing. Connie just shook her head and smiled, saying, "That's my "Bob"!"

The two then hugged and kissed in an almost normal manner — that is, until I noticed that their tongues were painfully poking at each others esophaguses as if they were in some sort of battle. This went on for fifteen minutes, exactly (I watched the clock on the wall), after which Mr. and Mrs. Dobbs went their own ways, ignoring each other as if nothing at all had happened. "Bob" grinned and gave a perverted grunt as he watched Connie walk away, then grabbed me by my wrist rather painfully and dragged me up a long flight of stairs.

It was then that I noticed that while the outside of the compound looked like a bunker, the inside looked pretty much exactly like the set of *Gone With The Wind*. By that I mean it *looked* like it, but half the furnishings were poorly built props. "Bob" gleefully demolished a well-painted but flimsy plywood armchair and when he noticed my bewilderment, giggled like a school girl and shoved my head through a thin plaster wall. I am not sure if he realized that just beyond the thin plaster was reinforced concrete.

We finally made it to his upstairs office. At the door were two fropped-out guards. One of them elbowed me in the ribs and maliciously snickered, "Bob's" gonna have some fun with you, boy!" Before, this would have disconcerted me, but by now I expected Mr. Dobbs to have "fun" with me any time he desired. If it weren't for the fact that I had a mission I would not have tolerated the abuse I had hence put up with... and I guess also for the fact that I was now somehow legally "Bob's" property.

We sat down on some comfortable easy chairs, both of us dazed, me from head trauma and "Bob" from God knows what. I found this latest office of "Bob's" more to my liking. It was simple, spartan and without any of his usual creepy knick-knacks about. "Bob" puffed away on his pipe while I took the time to relax. I could not be sure if he was contemplating something or if he was just zoning out. I suspect that he really does not think in the manner that we are accustomed to; rather, he just exists in the moment, a moment, any moment, and he simply does whatever feels the easiest.

The residual smoke from his pipe caused me to relax into a state which I believe may be akin to the one that the Hindoo Holy Men achieve when in a starvation-induced trance — or maybe "Bob's" Slack was just wearing off on me... for the longer he stared off into space, and I stared at his face, I began to feel this comforting disembodiment of self. "Bob" was in a trance and so was I... until he scared some feces out of me (into already ruined overalls, so I guess it didn't really matter at this point) by suddenly jumping up on his desk and very very loudly snapping his fingers, shouting, "I got it! I got it!" He bounded upon me and again painfully dragged me out of the room and into a large Hollywood-style costume dressing room. He giggled and giggled as he forced me to dress in a clownish cowboy outfit complete with bulbous, squeaking red nose, while he dressed himself in an authentic one. I knew that things were going to go downhill from here, at least until he Pil'd me up again.

Memo

May 15 1965 (?)

MR. Director,
I find myself on K. Atoll in the company of some of our men involved in the Nike-Zeus program. I am safe for now, it would seem. Although I am kept under quarantine, I am assured that I will soon be released. I am sending you this brief describing what I have seen and experienced to the best of my memory, which I am not sure I can trust any longer. I have been told the date, but even of that I cannot vouchsafe.

Mr. Director, I shall state this as plainly as possible. This Mr. Dobbs ("Bob" or "Jar" as his employees, or more honestly his fanatical adherents, call him) is most possibly the biggest threat to the freedom of the United States that we now face... or possibly our greatest ally and/or weapon. I beg you to read this brief with all credulity, insane as it may sound. I will only report to you in person some of the most grave and fantastical of the intelligence I have gathered. For now, I again beg you to make this "Bob" your TOP PRIORITY.

Agent _____

PS. Please arrange for the BEST of our plastic surgeons to be available on my arrival in the States proper.

Memo II

May 20, 1965

M R. Director,
This is the correct date. Everything has become clear in regards to your response.

In two days time I will be reporting to you in person.

Scrap the request for the surgeons. These are pretty spiffy. Just wait until you see them.

Agent _____

Buy *These* SubGenius Books!

Neighborworld

A bulldada science fiction novel by Lonesome Cowboy Dave DeLuca, the astounding improvisational wizard of The Church of the Sub-Genius radio show, "The Hour of Slack." A little bit *A Clockwork Orange*, a taste of The Firesign Theatre, a dab of Fleischer Brothers cartoons, a dash of Kafka, a splash of Fellini, and a whole fistful of Lonesome Cowboy Dave!

ISBN 9781946529008
218-page trade paperback for $14.99, Kindle for $6.99.

Book of the SubGenius

The "Sistine Chapel" of the 20th Century, this profusely illustrated, softbound Horror Bible, published by Simon & Schuster, is now in its 17th printing. You'll never have to read another book as long as you live–because you'll just sit, reading this one over and over again. Page after page of brain-raping text and graphics. A self-help book for sinners, creeps, morphodites, and all wise persons and guys who knew they wouldn't get "help" from any book even if they needed it in the first place.

ISBN 9781439188651
194-page trade paperback for $20.95

Eyelash

THE FIRST SUBGENIUS SCIENCE FICTION NOVEL! By Nikolai Kingsley. He swore he'd never deal with the aliens again, but here he was, letting them beam him onboard... He promised that whatever they were planning he'd keep Tai out of it, but here she was, on the bridge... What were the Xists trying to hide that was worse than Soul Harvesting and interstellar drug running, and why were they being so nice to him... at first?

ISBN 9781946529015
239-page trade paperback for $17.95

subgenius.com

JOIN THE CHURCH OF THE SUBGENIUS

The SubGenius material has only recently been made public. This is YOUR chance to get in on the ground floor of a huge, lucrative cult–NOW, while rates are low. You will then be eligible for all the $$$, weird sex, and SHEER POWER OVER OTHERS that go with high-ranking membership in the Church. And yes, YOU CAN PERFORM LEGAL WEDDINGS!

Overcome shyness and guilt with this fantastic replacement for a huge penis or "perfect" breasts. Read *THE STARK FIST OF REMOVAL* and learn not only the Word of Dobbs but also ways to contact, buy from, and sell to the incredible (yet real!!) network of SubGenii and subsymps everywhere. Learn of local revivals, other secret societies, UNUSUAL PRODUCTS, Other Mutants. THIS IS NO FAKE. Puts you "in charge" of your life. You'll be READY the next time your face is on fire. Quick Condown Clampspiracy release. Easy on delicate tissues... no danger of runaway infection.

This is the only way to get on the Mailing List of the Chosen, pierce the shroud of secrecy insulating the cult, join the secret MEMBERS-ONLY online forums and obtain such privileges as befit membership in a secret society of this scope. And all of it, including the surgery, can be done BY MAIL. Everything is kept STRICTLY CONFIDENTIAL (unless you want your local Clench listed). And don't worry about the diseases–they're part of the satire, too!

WHAT OTHER RELIGIONS CHARGE ALL WORLDLY GOODS FOR!!!

Be a Doktor INSTANTLY. Incredible, sinister super-miniaturized fine print details all the scores of Church Ranks and Titles from which YOU can CHOOSE.

Full of rants, art, Prescriptures, doctrine, charts, filth, comics, reviews and CHURCH NEWS & CONTACTS.

BE REBORN EVERY MINUTE!

HERE IS WHAT YOU *WILL* GET...

Pamphlets #1 & 2

Your Own Personal 8 x 11 inch suitable-for-framing DOBBSHEAD

Official Dobbshead / Church Logo Metal Pin

Dobbshead Sticker

Bumper Sticker

The SubGenius Pledge

The Divine Excuse (signed by "Bob!")

Doktorate of Forbidden Sciences

Propaganda flyers to copy

Stickers

Wallet sized, SubGenius MINISTER'S CARD

Minister's Ordination papers and instructions

The *STARK FIST of Removal* online

SCRUBGENIUS secret forum

dobbs.town - the SubGenius Mastodobbs

(Without that membership card you have NO HOPE on July 5th!!!)

SEND FIFTY DOLLARS TO:

The SubGenius Foundation
P.O. Box 807
Glen Rose, TX 76043
United States

subgenius.com

Welcome to Dobbstown

Meet or Avoid Other Superior Mutants

dobbs.town
dobbstown.org

www.ingramcontent.com/pod-product-compliance
Lightning Source LLC
Chambersburg PA
CBHW071125260626
47162CB00006B/2463

* 9 7 8 1 9 4 6 5 2 9 0 3 9 *